NEVER LOSE SIGHT OF THE DARK

Crazy Advice for Crazy Times

Daniel Wolf

PREFACE

A global pandemic, runaway inflation, food shortages, social and political upheaval, wars of aggression, rampant crime, climate change, and financial wrongdoing are among the major challenges we have faced in what seems to be one of the craziest periods in human history. We may seek to eliminate or at least mitigate these ills. However, we are aware of powerful forces that profit from political and social unraveling. Therefore, for many of us, the means of reversing or even merely containing such trends may be too formidable to contemplate.

While we await discovery of effective antidotes to these pressing issues, I propose, as a coping mechanism, a change of attitude to the many afflictions of modern society. The ancient Greek physician Hippocrates coined the saying "Desperate times require desperate measures." By way of analogy, I suggest that crazy times require crazy advice. Indeed, a humorous and ironical stance may better illuminate seemingly intractable problems. According to my book, "A distorted view of the world provides great clarity."

So in the absence of practical remedies, I hope my offering will provoke laughter or at least a few snickers. One item in the book states, "If you don't know where to go, you've found the right place." I might add that if you don't know what to read, you've found the right book.

Daniel Wolf

Learn from the past and stay there.

Judge not a man by his complete lack of intelligence or common sense.

If you did not hear someone's last words, ask him to repeat it.

If you are lost, lonely, aching, and homeless, prepare for bad luck.

Never lie to an electric blanket.

Money is no object unless it follows a verb.

Never trust a word with a silent letter. Clearly, *whole* is hiding something.

Learn to say no, especially if you stutter on the letter n.

Find someone kind, considerate, wise, supportive, positive, and intelligent—just don't tell your spouse.

Don't claim death is inevitable unless you can prove it.

Listen to your inner voice, but disregard that which is not grammatically correct.

Don't clamp down unless you actually own a set of clamps.

No man is an island. He's either a peninsula, an isthmus, or a strait.

A broken household appliance *is* the end of the world.

You are not the center of the universe; left of center, maybe.

Simple acts of kindness, strategically timed, can bring tremendous monetary reward.

A broken household appliance *is* the end of
the world.

Blame others for your miserable personality.

Think of death not as an end but as the beginning of a terrible day.

Call no man a coward. He will not hear you while running away.

Let others plan your life. They can do no worse.

You cannot escape your destiny, but try anyway.

Be yourself, though obviously, this is not a winning strategy.

Always blend in. Hiding is better.

Your family exists solely as an existential threat.

Have no fixed thoughts. Better yet, have no thoughts.

Be as ill-defined and bland as possible. A career in middle management awaits you.

Be as inconsistent and evasive as possible. A political career awaits you.

Demand respect even if you're wholly undeserving.

Don't respond to insults. There's a nastier one waiting if you do.

Go to bed early. You've experienced enough insanity for one day.

Don't bother learning from your mistakes. You're bound to repeat them anyway.

A distorted view of the world provides great clarity.

If you claim your pet is your best friend, you might need to work on your social skills.

Never lose sight of the dark.

Avoid people who know you.

Avoid people who like you.

What you lost, you never truly had—like your self-respect.

Distinguish yourself from your peers—wear a crazy hat.

Rehearse puppy eyes before an important job interview. If necessary, get on all fours and beg.

Hire only sycophants.

Distinguish yourself from your peers—wear a crazy hat.

If asked why you have no friends, explain that they all died in World War II.

Announce that you know everything — then leave.

When deciding upon a course of action, don't let trivialities, like your reputation, stand in the way.

You might want to work on your parenting skills if your toddler says, "It's my life and I'll do what I want."

Beware of sing-alongs.

Life is short. Dreams take time. Do the math.

Life is short. *Know thyself* takes time. Do the math.

Lie to yourself. It makes life worth living.

Never contradict a young person. Let life do it.

When taking out a date, never say, "The best things in life are free."

Be the first to arrive at the same conclusion.

Don't be content with idle gossip. Make your gossip come alive!

For heaven's sake—don't bring anyone new into your family.

Make yourself essential to every discussion—even if you know nothing about the topic.

When someone makes a clever remark, immediately respond, "You took the words right out of my mouth."

Give in to temptation. You've already given in to everything else.

Go where no man would even think of going.

Challenge yourself to a duel.

Don't let food be the center of your life. Beverages are important too.

Make a grand entrance even if no one is in the room.

Never forget to surprise yourself.

If undecided, ask yourself, "What would an indecisive person do?"

Reflect upon your life, then pursue with vengeance anyone who gave you advice.

Look up to yourself.

Make a grand entrance even if no one is in the room.

Anything worth doing will be difficult. Therefore, don't bother.

If a boss criticizes your job performance, remind him that your mission is to accomplish the impossible, not the possible.

Prepare for the remote possibility that you might succeed.

Never promise to show promise.

Attend only those conferences with tables that give away free pens, notepads, and keychains.

Respond to all criticism as a personal insult. The last thing you need is a meaningful discussion.

When asked "What's on your mind?" respond "Hair." Again, the last thing you need is a meaningful discussion.

Force people to like you.

A brief exchange is still too long.

You can be whatever others tell you to be.

Don't bother learning to lose. It will come naturally.

Love yourself, but don't forget foreplay.

When one door closes, another one's not far behind.

Don't let anyone ruin your day. Ruin it yourself.

If you didn't hear it the first time, you didn't
miss anything.

Don't conceal your ignorance. Revel in it!

When you have not a shred of dignity left, it's Miller time!

Stand aside during animal mating season.

Know your limits. It won't take long.

A new day dawns. Stay in bed.

When cornered, flee to a round room.

Speak truth to power lawnmowers.

If you're a chess enthusiast, avoid those with a
checkered past.

Support equity. Imagine where you'd rank without it.

S tand aside during animal mating season

Support diversity. Otherwise, people might think you look weird.

Never say, "My friend and I feed off each other" amongst cannibals.

Return to the scene of your greatest disappointment— unless you're already home.

Don't let constant, never-ending, round-the-clock failure affect your mood.

Do not confuse a pregnant pause with contraception.

If you have multiple personalities, be true to yourselves.

Not everything people say about you is true—but there's enough to convict.

Confuse everyone—be honest.

Don't let a goal stand in the way of a good excuse.

Choose a neighborhood that has few people but a bustling nightlife.

Never close a door on the unhinged.

Recoil in fear, then ask someone to unrecoil you.

Try to relive a near-death experience.

Confront the doctor who delivered you.

Buy a glass house, then throw stones at your neighbors. Record the result.

Confess your dreams only to those you won't see again. Otherwise, you'll constantly be asked, "Hey, whatever happened to that big dream of yours?"

A new day dawns. Stay in bed.

Beware the school principal who says, "Accept no substitute."

Beware the orthodontist who says, "Brace yourself."

Be generous with your time. Hand out clocks to everyone you meet.

If you can't be kind to animals, be kind to animal crackers.

There are no shortcuts in life except for hairstyles.

Never dare a daredevil.

Don't let well-informed, highly intelligent, experienced people influence you in any way.

"Don't breathe a word" is just an expression. Use your mouth for speaking.

Be generous with your time. Hand out clocks to everyone you meet.

Imagine how lonely the rich are. I can't either.

Nip crime in the bud — report those who take your breath away.

Try to resolve long-simmering disputes before the elevator doors open.

Setbacks are only a pause on the road to utter collapse.

There's no point organizing a movement against a symphony conductor.

Don't bother texting to someone from ancient times.

Imagine yourself in a foreign country. You can save on airfare, avoid losing luggage, and escape from annoying tourists.

Do not expect to lose weight by exercising restraint.

If you know you can do it, then don't bother.

A relationship built on suspicion, deception, trickery, and attempted murder cannot long endure.

If you cannot make friends naturally, see how much they cost.

Threaten anyone who does not appreciate the beauty of silence.

It's always darkest before the storm.

It's important to save face, though some faces are not worth saving.

If you wish to relive the past, at least take an umbrella.

Mathematicians seek the mean. They need to find nicer people.

Pay your Bills promptly. The Harrys can wait.

Harbor no ill will while touring a nuclear weapons facility.

Don't literally wrap your head around a problem.

Don't let the prospect of colliding galaxies interfere with your wedding plans.

Note any small changes in how mobs react to you.

Don't advertise your inadequacies. Reserve for others the pleasure of discovery.

Talk to nature, but don't argue.

Protecting yourself against the elements does not require memorizing the Periodic Table.

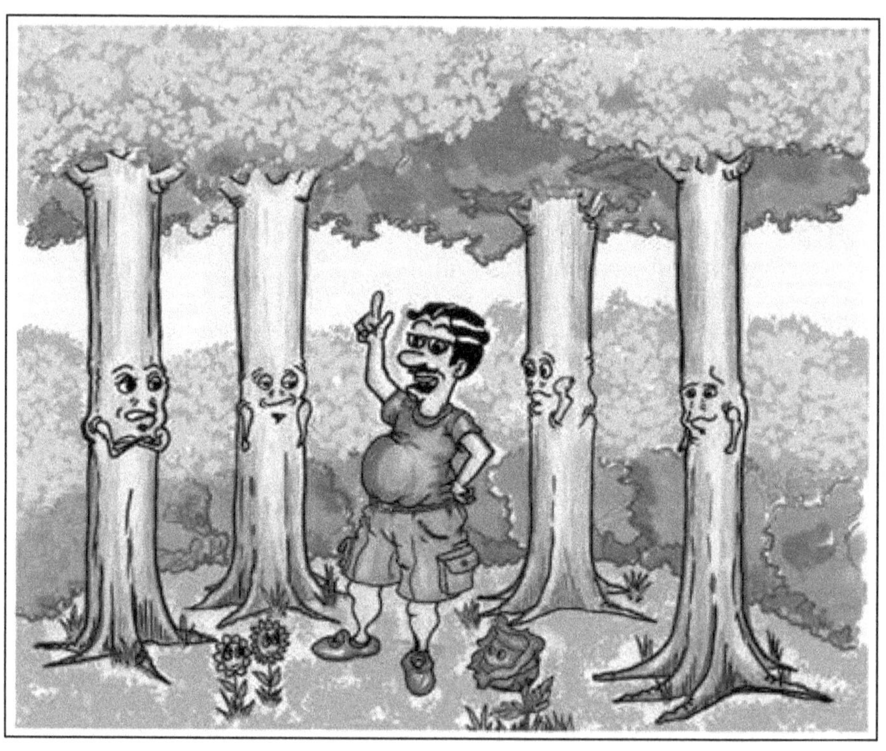

Talk to nature, but don't argue.

You can quit only what you have started. Until you start, you cannot quit.

"Do unto others" does not mean spilling Mountain Dew on someone.

If you wish to be alone, be annoying.

It's no great accomplishment to get rich while living. The trick is to get rich after you're gone.

Firmly state your intention to waver.

Don't be bothered by insults that penetrate the core of your being.

Wear a neck brace while running at breakneck speed.

If you are charged with a crime, a good defense is "I didn't ask to be born."

Take an advanced calculus exam outdoors because the answers are "blowing in the wind."

There's no point in trying to make a good impression on a sculptor.

If you have only yourself to thank, be coy about it.

Bless the children and other untamed creatures.

Beware of people who suddenly take up residence in your home.

A beverage company is not equipped to satisfy your thirst for knowledge.

Praise everyone to the rafters. You'll never spend a dime.

It's redundant to clown around at a circus.

Don't expect a family atmosphere at the billing
department.

Don't teach baseball players to error on the side
of caution.

No one suddenly becomes a jerk. It takes years of practice.

Don't beg to differ. You'll look ridiculous.

Wait until a solar eclipse has passed before casting a
shadow on current events.

Confess your love but not to a juror.

"I need to bone up on my studies" should never be uttered
in polite society.

As you reflect upon your life, keep sharp instruments at a
safe distance.

As you reflect upon your life, keep sharp instruments at a safe distance.

Seek permission before describing a time when you felt
truly free.

Though time is money, be yourself a few minutes a day.

Seniors should avoid the double take. An afterthought is
less stressful on the neck.

Nip crime in the bud—report furtive glances and
sneak peeks.

Know your options—speak with a financial advisor before
investing in yourself.

Rehearse your last words. Study method acting if
necessary.

Impart wisdom unto your children while their iPads are
recharging.

Never let a rapidly advancing horde interfere with
committee protocol.

A tortured soul doth not a good roommate make.

Losing a well-paying job should not deter you from entering the Publishers Clearinghouse Sweepstakes.

If you can't locate the child within you, consider posting an Amber Alert.

Thank God you're not part of a prayer circle.

Don't act the fool. *Be* a fool.

Don't believe anyone who claims to have had a sobering thought at a bar.

Care not what others say about you. If you're home and alone, you won't hear them.

If an airline loses your luggage, at least you will have lost weight.

Though there is much overlap, don't confuse situational awareness with situation comedy.

Maintain an emergency contact should you ever get lost in thought.

The truth shall set you free, but a prison break is more efficient.

Flaunt your flaws, but not in public.

Unburden yourself, but not in public.

Don't let good fortune ruin your naturally miserable disposition.

If you get thrown under the bus, tinker with the brakes.

Avoid the opposite sex. In most cases, it's a win-win.

I f you get thrown under the bus, tinker with the brakes.

Arrange to have your image on milk cartons if kidnapped by a notorious drug cartel.

There is no need to hide. No one is looking for you.

Recall all the fun you had when you were young, even if you must make it up.

Find fault with earthquakes, not people.

Never discourage an overly generous friend.

Respond to everyday events with gaping-mouth astonishment, though this might cause lockjaw.

Pray that accountants err in your favor.

Prank a space alien. They prank us

Don't believe everything you say.

Bring an extra set of clothes to a police lineup.

Check out the latest gadgetry if you wish to communicate from the grave.

Neither a lurker nor a leerer be.

Look confidently towards the future, especially if you've made a muck of the present.

Don't admit to your admirers that you're working into your nineties because you're flat-out broke.

No need to be at a certain place at the appointed time. If you don't show up, no one will notice.

Don't say "He's in a better place" at the funeral of someone who died while on his dream vacation.

Insist that people tell heartwarming tales about you.

Never sew discord among tailors.

Practice perking your ears.

Practice nodding in agreement.

Don't waste time being the best that you can be. You have more important things to do.

There is much to learn from lazy people, though they may not show up till evening.

Regale others with your complete lack of talent.

Don't step on someone's dream even if it's borderline psychotic.

Regale others with your complete lack of talent.

Just admit that you got laid off instead of saying you want to spend more time with your family.

Respond to all human misfortune with "Ouch!" After all, brevity is the soul of wit.

Inform your opponent of his weak point. He may show mercy.

If you want to be cool, surround yourself with socially awkward people.

Life is not a popularity contest. It's a beauty contest, and let's be honest …

Concede early. Why delay the inevitable?

Though humor helps create a relaxed working environment, mother jokes don't.

Cast your fate to the wind. Maybe that will work.

A wad of cash is more beautiful than a baby's smile.

Take heart—some still like you.

Fill each day with love and joy, though a job wouldn't hurt either.

Beware the slippery slope of chitchat. It could lead to spots on late-night television.

Respond to all reports of cataclysmic events with "That's a little more information than I need."

Learn how to vie. It will serve you well.

If you are not good at subtraction, no one will think less of you.

Listen to the unsuccessful. They are a font of great wisdom.

When planning a kidnapping, make sure somebody wants
the victim returned.

If salary depends on performance, see if tap
dancing counts.

Peace begins at home, which may or may not include
apartments.

Constantly monitor your financial situation while leading
a carefree life.

Being in the military does not entitle you to make a
waitress do ten push-ups if she gets the order wrong.

If required to sing for your supper, be sure the song is in
the public domain.

If a doctor says you have a terminal illness, he's not
referring to airports.

If you don't know where to go, you've found the
right place.

Constantly monitor your financial situation while leading a carefree life.

Ask an architect "What's your angle?" if you sense anything suspicious.

Force people to reminisce.

Never leave a party empty-handed.

The mind is unreliable. Use your sense of touch to know how you feel.

Add this to your bucket list: Create an uncomfortable silence.

There's no need to make a new friend. You already have enough headaches in your life.

Growing up in a household with one television is not a hardship. Losing the remote control is.

Greet each new day with "Oh no, not again."

There's no need to embellish your résumé. It's already overblown.

Join a winning team. They have more parties.

Make every conversation a comedy routine. Announce that your pronouns are *who, what, when, where,* and *why.*

Reaching middle age does not require you to compete in jousting tournaments.

If you use words such as *comfy, yummy,* and *tummy,* you're a *lunaticky.*

Wear your war face while taking a leisurely stroll at night.

When asked to do anything, respond with "I didn't sign up for this."

If you're a young adult, don't refer to yourself as *old school.*

Support the brave … by phone.

Add this to your bucket list: Continue a conversation long past its natural end.

If you want to relocate to a primitive society, prepare to be called Mister Know-It-All.

Learn how to dart when approaching someone you recognize.

Practice slinking away. It's a valuable skill if you're ever caught in a lie.

Beware of funeral directors who welcome you warmly.

Those born into wealth can skip Dress for Success.

When criticized, respond with "Guess I didn't get the memo on that."

B eware of funeral directors who welcome
you warmly.

Find out where your friends and family are going so you'll know what places to avoid.

Be a seeker of cash.

Pre-record "Yes" and "You're right" before calling someone who never stops talking.

Instead of saying "I wouldn't meet you if you were the last person on earth," say "We should get together sometime."

Avoid correcting a mafia don's spelling mistakes.

Never cry on a round shoulder. You might slide off.

Never lend money to anyone bigger than you.

It's not every day that one wakes up.

With all the problems occurring in the world, don't expect God to find time to be your witness.

If addition doesn't suffice when counting your blessings, use multiplication.

Never assume that the driver of a Mister Softee ice cream truck is impotent.

Question the sanity of a guidance counselor who claims that train conductor and orchestra conductor are essentially the same job.

Seasoned ballplayers do not need condiments.

Don't high-five anyone who is the sole survivor of a fiery plane crash.

If you can't get reparations, at least get Preparation H.

If you're a prizefighter, make sure your corner knows how to throw a towel.

Learn how to curse while studying to be a truck driver.

If inviting an astronaut into your home, make sure he has enough legroom.

Don't say "Let's go Dutch" to someone who had a bad experience in Holland.

Be a contrarian—let the door hit you on the way out.

Choose a company that schedules time to wallow in misery.

Don't "shout it from the rooftops". You could be in violation of a city ordinance.

Refer to everything you do, however trivial, as groundbreaking.

Test a famous saying. Destroy Rome, then try rebuilding it in a day.

Choose a company that schedules time to wallow in misery.

Be the giraffe in battle, the hippopotamus in surveillance, and the rhinoceros in negotiation. Naturally, this may require a constant change of clothing.

Be the lion in summer, though you'll need to make extra holes in the suit for ventilation.

Beware of butchers who want only a short-term relationship.

Don't blame your misfortune on the stars.
Blame the moon.

If you can't summon your courage, try bribing it.

Consult H&R Block when counting your blessings. There may be deductions.

The last thing you need is a worthy opponent.

American generals should not declare victory every time they leave a restaurant.

American generals should not declare victory every time they leave a restaurant.

If "It's not over till the fat lady sings," take an overweight soprano to a sporting event.

Be popular. You can always accomplish something later.

Don't give an alarm clock to anyone who views everything with alarm.

Be thankful for the little things in life. It should be obvious that the big things are not coming.

Don't forget to include an acute sense of smell on your résumé.

Act before thinking. Maybe that will work.

Don't make mountains out of molehills. Make mountain ranges.

Feign interest, concern, surprise … hell, fake everything.

Perform an honest day's work at least once a week.

Make a citizen's arrest of anyone who says, "Smile. It's not so bad."

"Our friendship is so strong that we hardly need to spend time together" means "I can't stand spending even a minute with this person."

If you want a cushy job, find a workplace with many sofas.

Demand identification before speaking with anyone, even your family.

You can learn much from observing animal behavior, but be careful where you scratch.

Planning a day with others in mind is a surefire path to disaster.

Make a rule, then violate it. Who are you to tell you what you can't do?

If you want a cushy job, find a workplace with many sofas.

Retracing your steps should not result in going
back to sleep.

Always be pleasant. No one needs to know what a raving
lunatic you really are.

A good excuse—don't leave home without it.

A petty grievance—don't leave home without it.

There's no need to "call your doctor immediately." They
will not answer.

For heaven's sake, send only a headshot if asked
for a photo.

Attend any event where there's free food.

It's better to succeed at something you enjoy doing than
fail at something you couldn't give a rat's ass about.

Test a friendship by revealing your dislike of a
mutual friend.

There is no such thing as a stupid question. There are only
stupid answers.

Litigate any perceived micro-aggression. Riches beyond
your wildest imagining await you.

If the American government considers your voice
annoying, speak with a British accent.

Encourage an escaped convict to visit his mother-in-law.
He will soon surrender to authorities.

Be Columbus—search the globe for a place that gives
away free stuff.

Challenge yourself—go where you're not welcome.

If someone says "I don't like the tone of your voice," respond with "I tone muscle, not voice."

Avoid joining a traveling circus that has to schnorr for gas money.

Speak up, especially if surrounded by professional basketball players.

Consider the possible consequences and implications before sending a get-well card.

There's little point in straightening your tie if you have lousy posture.

The ability to color-code your sock drawer may not be what employers are looking for at this time.

Try looking your best during life-and-death situations.

If nobody cares what you do, lead.

Speak up, especially if surrounded by professional basketball players.

Check your hair, make-up, and lighting before creating a public scene.

Support the rich. The government can do only so much.

The purpose of an express lane is to facilitate the purchase of goods, not to express your innermost thoughts and feelings to the cashier.

React with total indignation if anyone asks which of Snow White's seven dwarfs you most resemble.

When passing the ketchup, avoid waxing eloquent on the virtues of sharing.

Since celebrities often fake their death, fake your life.

Proudly ward off integrity: make your life a carbon copy of your parents'.

Be prepared to cite scripture to avoid something you don't want to do.

Withhold the benefit of the doubt from anyone whose stated goal is to make your life a living hell.

Arrange an intervention for anyone who seems well-adjusted.

If you're reputed to be a hero, work to eliminate your competition.

If you don't feel comfortable in your own skin, try switching with someone else.

Though everyone needs personal space, moving to a different time zone may be overdoing it.

Be careful not to awaken the giant within you. It'll eat everything.

Children should not operate heavy machinery, though a toddler driving an SUV is kind of cute.

If you're an itinerant worker, learn to say, "You can take this job and shove it" in different languages.

If you wish to retain many friends, never express how you truly feel about them.

Don't downplay your accomplishments. They're already at rock bottom.

Go tell it on the mountain. No one's listening to you here.

"Go with the flow" may not be the best option when approaching a waterfall.

Go overboard with gratitude. You'll never be asked to repay.

If we are nothing more than a collection of habits, stop everything!

Don't harangue someone who's just been harangued. Allow a few minutes for intermission.

Eschew any technology that does not control every facet of your waking life.

Go tell it on the mountain. No one's listening to you here.

Hard work will make you tired.

You cannot reason with carpenters. They never give an inch.

Give your family and friends a break—shorten the long face.

Forget casual Fridays if caught in a web of international intrigue.

Always give your audience a means of escape.

If exposed as a complete fraud, respond with "That's your opinion."

Don't let continual backstabbing ruin a working relationship.

Model yourself after somebody average. You won't be disappointed.

Express yourself, but make sure to include
enough postage.

Never follow advice that requires you to take action.

Take a few days off to recover from meeting others.

Consult a lawyer before opening your heart to someone.

Be generous. Let others take the blame.

Don't French kiss French fries. You could burn
your tongue.

Find yourself--but not in public.

Remain calm amongst those who twitch.

An inability to distinguish between "this dress" and "distress" could lead to dire consequences.

Never assume that the driver of a Good Humor ice cream truck has a pleasant personality.

Correct anyone who says "I have a theory." It's most likely a hypothesis, which is no more than a guess.

Be brave in word—then leave.

Don't forgo immediate gratification. There's no guarantee the opportunity will come again.

Defend your family—unless an attractive man or woman enters the picture.

If someone decides not to speak to you, you have much reason to celebrate.

If you wish to make others happy, tell them how unhappy *you* are.

Never assume that the driver of a Good Humor ice cream truck has a pleasant personality.

Don't expect much personal growth if trapped in a soul-crushing, lifeless, dry-as-dirt 9 to 5.

Test a popular expression. Place an elephant in a room and see if anyone notices it.

Say to yourself upon waking, "Today, I will meet ungrateful, uncaring, self-absorbed, and hyper-sensitive people." Then greet your family.

Name your pet "Peeve."

Don't sever a relationship during a trapeze performance.

Never buy a cute dog. You'll risk owning a publicity hound.

Change your scene. It's easier than changing your self.

Ensure you have the go-ahead before using the term "go-ahead."

Test a popular expression. Place an elephant in a room and see if anyone notices it.

First to arrive and last to leave will win you few friends at the workplace.

Don't expect to make friends at an aquarium. Fish have little time for social interaction.

Don't let people stick barbs in you unless your name is Barbara.

Go pirate—amass filthy lucre.

If you catch yourself doing all the talking, find someone to talk to.

When asked to define yourself, there's no need to mention hairlessness and bipedalism.

Make sure your watch is analogue before saying, "You have ten seconds to hand it over."

If you have almost all the money in the world, find the holdouts.

Those endowed with a booming voice should still
consider using telephones.

Since laughter is contagious, petition the government to
develop a vaccine.

If you want to look thin, make your house a Hall
of Mirrors.

Don't say your trigger words are work and responsibility
during a job interview.

If children are the future, ask them to come back later.

Expect much of others. Maybe someone in a galaxy far, far
away will hear you.

Nip crime in the bud. Report those who steal the covers
or engage in pillow fights.

Don't try to humor an angry comic.

If you want to look thin, make your house a Hall of Mirrors.

Before embarking on your life's journey, consider
not going.

Though you occupy both time and space, prepare to give
up one if necessary.

Don't confuse a horse's neigh with a "no" vote.

Test a popular expression. Spill milk on someone. Record
the result.

The failure to distinguish between bargain hunters and
big-game hunters could have tragic consequences.

Don't go where others fear to tread.

Be courageous when confronting imaginary enemies.

Confuse everyone—say you're a happy camper.

Arrange to arrive after an emergency has passed.

Engage in deep, personal communication through texting.

Excel at something no one has ever heard of.

Don't be deceived by cows. They're not as content as they seem.

If a soldier, lead the retreat.

Before joining a street gang, make sure it provides nap pods, cooking classes, and free laundry service.

Unless you're a martial artist, avoid the crowd surrounding the buffet table.

Sleep with confidence.